Sister Day!

For the Manchevs, who brought a whole new set
of sisters (and brothers) into my life—L. M.

To my family and friends, especially to my aunt Dolores—S. S.

SIMON & SCHUSTER BOOKS FOR YOUNG READERS
An imprint of Simon & Schuster Children's Publishing Division
1230 Avenue of the Americas, New York, New York 10020
Text copyright © 2017 by Lisa Mantchev
Illustrations copyright © 2017 by Sonia Sánchez Martinez
All rights reserved, including the right of reproduction in whole or in part in any form.
SIMON & SCHUSTER BOOKS FOR YOUNG READERS is a trademark of Simon & Schuster, Inc.
For information about special discounts for bulk purchases,
please contact Simon & Schuster Special Sales
at 1-866-506-1949 or business@simonandschuster.com.
The Simon & Schuster Speakers Bureau can bring authors to your live event.
For more information or to book an event,
contact the Simon & Schuster Speakers Bureau at 1-866-248-3049 or visit our website at www.simonspeakers.com.
Book design by Laurent Linn
The text for this book is set in ITC Highlander Std.
The illustrations for this book are rendered digitally.
Manufactured in China
0317 SCP
First Edition
2 4 6 8 10 9 7 5 3 1
Library of Congress Cataloging-in-Publication Data
Names: Mantchev, Lisa. | Sánchez, Sonia, 1983– illustrator.
Title: Sister Day! / Lisa Mantchev ; illustrated by Sonia Sánchez.
Description: First edition. | New York : Simon & Schuster Books for Young Readers, [2017] | "A Paula Wiseman Book." |
Summary: When her big sister is too busy to play "Let's pretend" and tell entertaining stories, a little sister creates Sister Day.
Identifiers: LCCN 2014030182| ISBN 9781481437950 (hard cover) | ISBN 9781481437967 (eBook)
Subjects: | CYAC: Sisters—Fiction.
Classification: LCC PZ7.M31827 Si 2017 | DDC [E]—dc23
LC record available at https://lccn.loc.gov/2014030182

Sister Day!

BY **Lisa Mantchev**

ILLUSTRATED BY **Sonia Sánchez**

A Paula Wiseman Book
Simon & Schuster Books for Young Readers
New York London Toronto Sydney New Delhi

My big sister, Jane, has the best imagination. She makes up all kinds of things out of her very own head.

"Want to dress up and pretend something?"

"Not right now, Lizzie," says Jane.

"Tell me a story?" I ask. "The one where I'm not really your sister because you found me in the garden under a rock."

"I can't," she says. "I'm going to Emma's house for a play date."

"When you get home?" I ask.

"Maybe when I get home."

That evening I wait for Jane to come home.

And I wait.

And I wait some more.

I hear a car pull up outside. Jane's home!

"Want to tell stories in my fort?" I ask. "I used *all* the blankets!"

Jane shakes her head. "Mom said I had to do my homework."

"You're always busy."

The next morning I point to the only empty box on her calendar. "What day is this?"

"That's Saturday," she says.

I have an idea, an idea for a grand, glorious, practically perfect surprise. I find my pink crayon and circle, circle, circle that Saturday.

On Monday Jane has soccer practice. Instead of
cheering, I get to work because dragons are tricky.

On Tuesday Jane goes to ballet. Usually I like to jump and twirl too, but today I have to put tutus on sugarplum fairies.

Piano lessons are on Wednesday. The metronome goes *click! clack! click! clack!* while I get the orchestra in place.

Karate is on Thursday. While Jane practices kicking,
I practice sneaking. I *sneak! sneak! sneak!* to a quiet
corner to finish up my surprise.

Friday afternoon Jane goes to Emma's house again. Mom helps me bake Jane's favorite treat.

Early the next morning I get out my sketchbook and my roll of Scotch tape and my scissors. It takes an hour and the whole roll of tape, but when everything is ready, I go up to Jane's room.

I remember to knock.
Knock, knock, knock!
"Jane?"
No answer.
Even though I'm not
supposed to, I open the door.
Her room is *empty*.

I run downstairs yelling,

"Mom, have you seen Jane!?"

But when I turn the corner to the kitchen, Jane is standing there wearing a T-shirt covered in glittery glue.

"I made these for us at Emma's house," she says.

"They are perfect!" I clap my hands, wriggle into my shirt, and tug her into the living room.

"Surprise! I drew *you* a story!"
I say. "Happy Sister Day!"

"You didn't just draw a story, Lizzie," Jane says. "You made a whole lot of magic. You have a great imagination."

"It runs in the family," I tell her.